P9-CLE-439

SHE'LL BE COMING AROUND THE MOUNTAIN

Retold by BLAKE HOENA

Illustrated by ELLEN STUBBINGS

CANTATA
LEARNING

WWW.CANTATALEARNING.COM

CANTATA
LEARNING

Published by Cantata Learning
1710 Roe Crest Drive
North Mankato, MN 56003
www.cantatalearning.com

Copyright © 2016 Cantata Learning

All rights reserved. No part of this publication may be reproduced
in any form without written permission from the publisher.

Library of Congress Control Number: 2015932817
Hoena, Blake
    She'll Be Coming Around the Mountain / retold by Blake Hoena; Illustrated
by Ellen Stubbings
    Series: Tangled Tunes
    Audience: Ages: 3–8; Grades: PreK–3
    Summary: In this lively twist on the classic song "She'll Be Coming Around
the Mountain," a rodeo clown tries to round up a wily old billy goat.
    ISBN: 978-1-63290-362-4 (library binding/CD)
    ISBN: 978-1-63290-493-5 (paperback/CD)
    ISBN: 978-1-63290-523-9 (paperback)
    1. Stories in rhyme. 2. Rodeos—fiction. 3. Billy goats—fiction.

Book design and art direction, Tim Palin Creative
Editorial direction, Flat Sole Studio
Music direction, Elizabeth Draper
Music produced by Erik Koskinen and recorded at Real Phonic Studios

Printed in the United States of America in North Mankato, Minnesota.
122015   0326CGS16

ACCESS THE MUSIC!

SCAN CODE WITH MOBILE APP

CANTATALEARNING.COM

Being a **rodeo** clown sure is hard work, especially for the girl in this story. She has a billy goat that she needs to **round up**. The girl and the goat chase each other around and around.

To see what happens, turn the page and sing along!

She'll be coming around the mountain when she comes.

(Yee haw!)

She'll be coming around the mountain when she comes.

She'll be coming around the mountain,
    she'll be coming around the mountain.

She'll be coming around the mountain when
    she comes.

(Yee haw!)

She'll round up a billy goat on the loose.

(Na-a-a-a, na-a-a-a!)

She'll round up a billy goat on the loose.

She'll round up a billy goat,

   she'll round up a billy goat.

She'll round up a billy goat on the loose.

   (Na-a-a-a, na-a-a-a!)

She'll have a painted face with a smile.

(Say cheese!)

She'll have a painted face with a smile.

She'll have a painted face,
  she'll have a painted face.
She'll have a painted face with a smile.
  (Say cheese!)

She'll wear a round red ball on her nose.
   (Honk, honk!)
She'll wear a round red ball on her nose.

She'll wear a round red ball,
   she'll wear a round red ball.
She'll wear a round red ball on her nose.
   (Honk, honk!)

15

She'll have on **floppy** shoes when she runs.

(Squeak, squeak!)

She'll have on floppy shoes when she runs.

She'll have on floppy shoes,
she'll have on floppy shoes.
She'll have on floppy shoes when she runs.
(Squeak, squeak!)

She'll **dive** into a **barrel** when she hides.

(Whoosh!)

She'll dive into a barrel when she hides.

18

She'll dive into a barrel,
   she'll dive into a barrel.
She'll dive into a barrel when she hides.
   (Whoosh!)

She'll be coming around the
mountain when she comes.
(Yee haw!)
She'll be coming around the
mountain when she comes.

She'll be coming around the mountain,
  she'll be coming around the mountain.
She'll be coming around the mountain
  when she comes.
  (Yee haw!)

SONG LYRICS
She'll Be Coming Around the Mountain

She'll be coming around the mountain when she comes.
  (Yee haw!)
She'll be coming around the mountain when she comes.

She'll be coming around the mountain,
  she'll be coming around the mountain.
She'll be coming around the mountain when she comes.
  (Yee haw!)

She'll round up a billy goat on the loose.
  (Na-a-a-a, na-a-a-a!)
She'll round up a billy goat on the loose.

She'll round up a billy goat,
  she'll round up a billy goat.
She'll round up a billy goat on the loose.
  (Na-a-a-a, na-a-a-a!)

She'll have a painted face with a smile.
  (Say cheese!)
She'll have a painted face with a smile.

She'll have a painted face,
  she'll have a painted face.
She'll have a painted face with a smile.
  (Say cheese!)

She'll wear a round red ball on her nose.
  (Honk, honk!)
She'll wear a round red ball on her nose.

She'll wear a round red ball,
  she'll wear a round red ball.
She'll wear a round red ball on her nose.
  (Honk, honk!)

She'll have on floppy shoes when she runs.
  (Squeak, squeak!)
She'll have on floppy shoes when she runs.

She'll have on floppy shoes,
  she'll have on floppy shoes.
She'll have on floppy shoes when she runs.
  (Squeak, squeak!)

She'll dive into a barrel when she hides.
  (Whoosh!)
She'll dive into a barrel when she hides.

She'll dive into a barrel,
  she'll dive into a barrel.
She'll dive into a barrel when she hides.
  (Whoosh!)

She'll be coming around the mountain when she comes.
  (Yee haw!)
She'll be coming around the mountain when she comes.

She'll be coming around the mountain,
  she'll be coming around the mountain.
She'll be coming around the mountain when she comes.
  (Yee haw!)

She'll Be Coming Around the Mountain

Americana
Erik Koskinen

1. She'll be com-ing a-round the moun-tain when she comes. (Yee haw!) She'll be com-ing a-round the moun-tain when she comes. She'll be com-ing a-round the moun-tain, she'll be com-ing a-round the moun-tain. She'll be com-ing a-round the moun-tain when she comes. (Yee haw!)

Verse 2
She'll round up a billy goat on the loose.
 (Na-a-a-a, na-a-a-a!)
She'll round up a billy goat on the loose.

She'll round up a billy goat,
 she'll round up a billy goat.
She'll round up a billy goat on the loose.
 (Na-a-a-a, na-a-a-a!)

Verse 3
She'll have a painted face with a smile.
 (Say cheese!)
She'll have a painted face with a smile.

She'll have a painted face,
 she'll have a painted face.
She'll have a painted face with a smile.
 (Say cheese!)

Verse 4
She'll wear a round red ball on her nose.
 (Honk, honk!)
She'll wear a round red ball on her nose.

She'll wear a round red ball,
 she'll wear a round red ball.
She'll wear a round red ball on her nose.
 (Honk, honk!)

Verse 5
She'll have on floppy shoes when she runs.
 (Squeak, squeak!)
She'll have on floppy shoes when she runs.

She'll have on floppy shoes,
 she'll have on floppy shoes.
She'll have on floppy shoes when she runs.
 (Squeak, squeak!)

Verse 6
She'll dive into a barrel when she hides.
 (Whoosh!)
She'll dive into a barrel when she hides.

She'll dive into a barrel,
 she'll dive into a barrel.
She'll dive into a barrel when she hides.
 (Whoosh!)

Verse 7
She'll be coming around the mountain when she comes.
 (Yee haw!)
She'll be coming around the mountain when she comes.

She'll be coming around the mountain,
 she'll be coming around the mountain.
She'll be coming around the mountain when she comes.
 (Yee haw!)

ACCESS THE MUSIC!
SCAN CODE WITH MOBILE APP
CANTATALEARNING.COM

23

GLOSSARY

barrel—a round, wooden container

dive—to jump headfirst

floppy—soft and easy to move

rodeo—a contest or show featuring cowboys and cowgirls and animals

round up—to gather an animal or animals

GUIDED READING ACTIVITIES

1. The setting in this story is a rodeo. What do you think a rodeo is? Have you ever seen one?

2. The girl is dressed as a clown and chasing a billy goat. Where else might you see clowns? Where else might you see billy goats?

3. Can you draw or paint a silly clown? What color is the clown's hair? What is the clown wearing? Describe your clown's face.

TO LEARN MORE

Gordon, Nick. *Rodeo Clown*. Minneapolis, MN: Torque, 2013.

Gowar, Mick. *Rodeo Rider*. North Mankato, MN: Capstone Press, 2013.

Janni, Rebecca. *Every Cowgirl Loves a Rodeo*. New York: Dial, 2012.

Peschke, Marci. *Kylie Jean Rodeo Queen*. North Mankato, MN: Picture Window Books, 2011.